GREENWICKS

LEXI'S STORY

Written by Adam and Charlotte Guillain

Illustrated by Katie Kear

RISING ★ STARS

Hachette UK's policy is to use papers that are natural, renewable and recyclable products and made from wood grown in well-managed forests and other controlled sources. The logging and manufacturing processes are expected to conform to the environmental regulations of the country of origin.

ISBN: 9781398324299

Text © Adam and Charlotte Guillain
Illustrations, design and layout © Hodder and Stoughton Ltd
First published in 2022 by Hodder & Stoughton Limited (for its Rising Stars imprint, part of the Hodder Education Group),
An Hachette UK Company
Carmelite House 50 Victoria Embankment London EC4Y 0DZ
www.risingstars-uk.com

Impression number 10 9 8 7 6 5 4 3 2 1
Year 2026 2025 2024 2023 2022

Author: Adam and Charlotte Guillain
Series Editor: Tony Bradman
Commissioning Editor: Hamish Baxter
Illustrator: Katie Kear/Bright International Group
Educational Reviewer: Helen Marron
Design concept: David Bates
Page layouts: Rocket Design (East Anglia) Ltd
Editor: Amy Tyrer

With thanks to the schools that took part in the development of *Reading Planet* KS2, including: Ancaster CE Primary School, Ancaster; Downsway Primary School, Reading; Ferry Lane Primary School, London; Foxborough Primary School, Slough; Griffin Park Primary School, Blackburn; St Barnabas CE First & Middle School, Pershore; Tranmoor Primary School, Doncaster; and Wilton CE Primary School, Wilton.

A catalogue record for this title is available from the British Library.

Printed in the United Kingdom

Orders: Please contact Hachette UK Distribution, Hely Hutchinson Centre, Milton Road, Didcot, Oxfordshire, OX11 7HH.

Telephone: (44) 01235 400555. Email: primary@hachette.co.uk.

MIX
Paper from
responsible sources
FSC™ C104740

Contents

1 A Chance for Lexi

"Boo!" shouted Lexi as she pelted past her friend.

"I heard you coming!" Sara laughed, running to catch up. "I'm on to you, Lexi."

Lexi and Sara hadn't been friends before their teacher Mr Ali put them in a reading group together at the start of the year. Surprisingly, Year 6 was going much better than Lexi had expected. At least, at school.

"Got you," gasped Sara, when she finally caught up with Lexi by the school gate.

Mrs Wilde, the headteacher at Greenwicks Primary School, was standing in the playground to welcome everyone, wearing a sharp blue suit with matching shoes.

"Good morning, Lexi. Good morning Sara," she said. "Lexi, I think Miss Barton is going to tell you about some big plans she has for you this term. Now in you go."

"What do you think she was on about?" asked Sara as they hurried in.

"Who knows?" said Lexi. "Greenwicks probably wants me to start scoring more goals for the school football team or something." But secretly she felt a flicker of curiosity and excitement as she wondered what it might be.

Mr Ali had set up lots of routines for his Year 6 class, meaning that Lexi and Sara were soon on their Monday morning trip to the library with the rest of their reading group.

"Good morning," said Mrs Warner, the librarian, who was sitting at her desk. "Carter, we have some new books on rap music, and Lexi, there are a couple of new sports titles, too."

The group were soon searching the shelves for books. Lexi was distracted though, wondering what Mrs Wilde had meant about Miss Barton's plans for her this term. Were the girls going to finally break away from the boys and start their own football team? The thought of this filled Lexi with hope. If they did that, Miss Barton might make her team captain. Surely then her mum and dad would want to come and watch her play?

"Carter, remember when you got to stand up and rap in assembly?" Sara asked Carter.

"That was so scary," said Carter, his eyes wide. "But amazing."

"I can do something amazing too," said Lexi. "Watch this!"

Lexi took a short run up and somersaulted into a big pile of beanbags.

Everyone cheered.

"Now me!" called Sara, tightening her hijab.

Sara's attempt at a somersault didn't quite go to plan and she collided with a rotating book display.

"That's enough!" called Mrs Warner crossly. "I'm going to have to speak to Mr Ali about this group." She looked across at Lexi, who was hunting around for her fallen hearing aid while sniggering.

"Lexi, help Sara tidy up that book display, please," she said.

"She didn't mean to knock it over," said Carter. "And anyway, it was funny."

"Carter, that kind of immature attitude will get you into a lot of trouble next year at secondary school," Mrs Warner warned him before going back to her work.

"I wish I could somersault like that," said Femi, poking a beanbag with his foot.

"Do you think any of us will go to the same secondary school?" said Sara as she gathered up the scattered books.

"Who knows?" said Lexi. "I don't think my mum and dad have even thought about where I should go next year. Crown Woods sounds best for sports, I think."

"I don't want to go to any of the choices my mum's been talking about," said Femi gloomily. "Not without any of you, anyway."

Everyone was silent then, lost in their own worries about secondary school.

Later that morning, Miss Barton took Year 6 for PE in the hall and Lexi finally found out what her teacher's plans for her were.

"Exciting news! Next month I'll be taking six girls and six boys from Years 5 and 6 to a big inter-school gymnastics competition," she told the class.

Lexi stopped trying to make Femi laugh by blowing on the back of his head and quickly tuned in.

Miss Barton asked for anyone who was interested to put their hand up.

"Go for it!" Sara hissed, giving Lexi a nudge.

Lexi's body stiffened as hands shot up around her. Last year she'd been going to a gymnastics club three times a week, and she'd have put her hand up in a flash.

"Lexi, what about you?" Miss Barton asked.

Lexi sensed everyone was looking at her, expecting her to put up her hand.

"Maybe," she said quietly. Since her dad had lost his job and the twins were born, there just hadn't been the money or time for Lexi's gymnastics. Was she still any good at it?

Miss Barton soon had the class working hard on the apparatus. At one point, she asked Lexi to demonstrate the safest way to climb the wall bars.

Just then Mrs Wilde passed through the hall with a man who caught everyone's attention.

Their headteacher was always showing visitors around. Most weren't interesting, but this man was extremely tall and wore a red tracksuit with very cool trainers.

"I bet he plays professional basketball," Ryan whispered to Carter.

As he passed through the hall, the man smiled at the children.

"That was an excellent demonstration," he said to Lexi with a friendly wave.

Miss Barton gave Lexi a smile which made her feel a bit awkward.

"Excuse me, are you famous?" Carter blurted.

Mrs Wilde stopped and turned around.

"Greenwicks pupils don't call out now, do they?" she said, narrowing her eyes at Carter.

"Carter does," Lexi muttered.

Quite a few children giggled and Lexi thought she was going to get told off but then Miss Barton interrupted them.

"I think our visitor might like to know that Lexi is our star gymnast," she said, pointing up at the high bars. "We're hoping she's going to lead our gymnastics team in this year's inter-school competition in London."

Lexi was shocked. What? Miss Barton wanted her to lead the team? She hadn't even volunteered yet.

"Well, from what I've just seen, I think you'd do a great job, Lexi," said the man. "Good luck with the competition!"

Another compliment! Lexi felt embarrassed, scared and excited all at once.

Lexi had always felt that PE was her thing. She was good at everything: ball games, athletics, dance. If she really could help the school gymnastics team do well in the competition then her parents might remember how good at sports she was. Finally, everyone, even her mum and dad, would see that she could do more than just muck about and make people laugh.

"So, Lexi, is that a yes?" asked Miss Barton with a twinkle in her eye.

Lexi glanced at the mystery visitor who seemed as interested as everyone else.

"Okay," she said.

"Good," Miss Barton said with a smile. The man gave Lexi a quick thumbs up before following Mrs Wilde out of the hall.

2 New Girl in Class

It didn't take long for Miss Barton to start the after-school practice sessions for the gymnastics competition. There weren't quite enough girls, but Lexi wondered if that meant the five who had volunteered would just do a bit more.

When Lexi started practising cartwheels on the school field at breaktimes, lots of children in other classes wanted to join in.

"You're practically a celebrity to Year 3," said Carter, as Lexi and her friends met for a chat one lunchtime. "Have you seen the way they all watch you and try to join in?"

"So, how's it going?" asked Femi. "What have you actually got to do in the competition?"

"We've all got to perform in four events," Lexi told her friends.

"I think Miss Barton's hoping I can win an individual medal with my floor routine. If the others do a good job, we might even win a medal in the overall team event."

"You're brilliant on the mat," said Femi. "No one can do all that upside down flippy stuff like you."

"I'm working on an amazing end to my floor routine," said Lexi. "I'll finish with a straddle jump into an aerial cartwheel. Miss Barton thinks if I can nail the landing, I'll get the points to win the individual medal, which will really help the team, too!"

"You've been going to a gymnastics club for years, right?" said Carter. "So, you're bound to be better than everyone else."

Sara shot a look at Carter. It was the kind of look that said, Stop talking – NOW!

"What?" said Carter. "I'm just saying."

Lexi stared at the ground and folded her arms.

"I stopped going to that club ages ago," she mumbled. "It was too far away."

"But why?" exclaimed Carter. "You love gymnastics! Like I love Mr Ali's singing club and I'm never going to stop going to that!"

"She can't go," said Sara, glancing at Lexi to check it was okay to tell the others.

"My dad lost his job," Lexi mumbled.

Lexi went on, "We had to sell the car and since the twins were born there's no money to pay for extra stuff like club fees or taxis to get there."

"Oh," said Carter.

No one spoke for a moment.

"Sorry, Lexi," said Femi.

"Well, you should definitely go and win this thing then," Carter told Lexi. "When everyone sees how amazing you are, your mum and dad will have to find some way of making that club thing happen for you again."

Lexi didn't hold out any hope of that happening. Money was really tight for her family these days and the twins always seemed to need so many things.

Lexi didn't tell the others but she knew her mum and dad had started going to the local food bank when money was tight. But she did think it would be nice if one of them at least could come and watch her do well in the gymnastics competition. With all the time the twins were taking up, her parents hardly noticed her at all any more!

"You could definitely win a medal, Lexi," said Femi.

"Yeah, you could," said Sara.

"And we're all coming to watch you do it, right?" said Carter.

Everyone started talking excitedly at once. Lexi grinned. It was fantastic to have friends who knew what mattered to you. Even the sad stuff that got you down.

Part of Lexi wanted to thank her friends for supporting her.

But she also felt a bit embarrassed, so she blew the biggest, longest, loudest raspberry that she could instead. Everyone laughed.

"Raspberry-blowing is a competition Lexi would definitely win," said Sara, grinning.

Lexi's feelings of hope and excitement were still there the next day. But then she got a shock. She had barely sat down in her chair for morning registration, when Mrs Wilde appeared in the doorway. Next to her was a girl Lexi hadn't seen for months.

"Everyone, can I have your attention please for a moment?" said Mr Ali, welcoming Mrs Wilde and the girl into the room.

"I'd like you all to welcome Dina-May," said Mr Ali with a smile. "She's joining our class from today. I know you'll all make her feel welcome."

"Lexi, what's up?" asked Femi, seeing the shock on her face. "Do you know her?"

Know her? Dina-May went to the same gymnastics club that Lexi used to go to. Dina-May won practically everything. Her bedroom was probably a treasure trove of medals and trophies. Why had she moved to Greenwicks Primary now? Just when Lexi was trying to make her mark as the best gymnast in the school?

Lexi's head filled with worried thoughts as Dina-May sat down and the lesson started.

"Lexi?" said Mr Ali.

Lexi was vaguely aware that Mr Ali had been trying to teach something but she had been too lost in her thoughts to listen.

"So, Lexi, how would you tackle that question?" asked Mr Ali patiently.

Question? What question? Usually, if she got stuck, Lexi would try to find something funny to say. Or pretend her hearing aid wasn't working. Today, she was just stuck for words. Luckily, Femi stepped in with an answer and saved her skin.

All through that afternoon's maths lesson, Lexi kept glancing across at Dina-May. Lexi couldn't quite believe she was really there, in her class. One time, Dina-May caught Lexi looking and gave her a smile and a wave. Lexi was mortified.

"You idiot!" she told herself. "Now she knows I recognise her and will want to talk to me!"

Somehow, Lexi got through the afternoon and into Miss Barton's after-school gymnastics session without having to talk to anyone.

"You were weird this afternoon," said Brianna as they started their warm-up on the mats.

"What do you mean?" snapped Lexi.

"Well, to start with you were sitting there like a lemon not saying anything when Mr Ali asked you that question," said Brianna. "Then you kept staring at Dina-May like she was being the strange one! Do you know her or something?"

"She used to go to my old gymnastics club," said Lexi, matter-of-factly. "She's snooty."

"I thought she seemed really nice," said Brianna, sounding surprised.

Lexi shrugged. Dina-May had always been in the top group at the club, which meant they'd hardly ever trained together. For all Lexi knew, Dina-May had no idea she even existed. But then, Dina-May had smiled and waved at her in class. All this was going on in Lexi's head as Dina-May came into the hall.

What? Lexi thought. *She's only been here five minutes. How come she's here at team practice already?*

Lexi was relieved when Miss Barton asked Dina-May to join some Year 5 girls practising their beam exercises. Then the teacher's attention went back to Lexi and the other children working on their floor routines.

"Lexi, you're doing brilliantly!" said Miss Barton, when Lexi nailed her final aerial.

"If you can land that perfectly on the day, I think you have a good chance of a medal," Miss Barton added.

At the end of the session, as they headed out, Dina-May called over, "Hi, Lexi."

But Lexi pretended she didn't hear and ran out of the hall.

That night, Lexi couldn't sleep. She thought of all the sessions she'd missed since she'd had to give up gymnastics club. If the other competitors in the gymnastics competition all went to after-school clubs, she had no chance of winning anything. Why did her dad have to lose his job? It wasn't fair.

The next day, Lexi was in a terrible mood at school and couldn't stop yawning. In PE, Miss Barton chose Dina-May to demonstrate the perfect run-up to a vault. Lexi sighed loudly and stared out of the window. She didn't clap Dina-May for her effort, even though everyone else in the class did.

Miss Barton spoke to Lexi after the lesson.

"Lexi, I know it's been hard for you since the twins were born. And it's been really tough for your mum and dad," Miss Barton started.

Lexi was shocked. She hadn't expected Miss Barton to talk about this and wanted her to stop – right now!

"I know they're not able to get you to the gymnastics club at the moment," said Miss Barton.

"I'm sure that's very difficult and disappointing for you," she went on.

"But, Lexi, you have a natural ability and being mean-spirited about Dina-May joining the team isn't like you. With hard work and focus you could do really well in this competition. Now, how about welcoming Dina-May to the team and helping her make some new friends? Come on, what do you say?"

Lexi stared at the floor. "Okay," she muttered.

But Lexi wasn't okay. Not one bit. She was a ticking time bomb of 'not-okay'. Especially at lunchtime, when she saw Dina-May eating with Sara, Carter and Femi. Lexi went off in a huff to sit at a table with some Year 5 boys she didn't even know.

When her friends all went out to the field together, Lexi stormed over to the outside apparatus and started practising bits of her bar routine.

"You're looking a bit upset, Lexi," said Femi, who wandered over when she finally sat down for a rest.

"I'm not upset!" snapped Lexi.

Even as she said it, she knew that she was.

"You didn't sit with us at lunch," said Femi. "How come?"

"You were all sitting with that snooty new girl," growled Lexi.

"She's not snooty. She's a bit shy but she's quite funny," said Femi. "She says she recognises you from gym club and that you're really good. She said she hasn't had a chance to talk to you yet because you're always so busy."

Lexi noticed Sara and Carter were coming over to join them now and she felt her anger bubbling up inside.

"Hey, Lexi, come and teach us how to do aerials. Dina-May says you're the best," called Sara.

"Me?" shouted Lexi. "If you want to learn how to do an aerial, ask Dina-May. She's the best at everything – didn't you know?"

"Lexi, why are you so angry with us all?" asked Carter.

"Because now you're all like, 'Dina-May *this* and Dina-May *that*' and no one even cares how I feel about anything!"

"Yes we do!" said Sara.

"I'm going," said Carter. "This is pointless."

"You can all go!" Lexi bellowed, wildly throwing out an arm. "Leave me alone!"

28

Unfortunately, Lexi's hand caught Sara's face as she turned, knocking her glasses to the ground. Lexi's friends gasped as Sara crouched down to pick the glasses up.

Lexi stormed off to the girls' toilets, unaware of what she'd done. Slamming the door to the cubicle inside, she pushed her hands on to her face and tried to force back the storm inside her head.

First, all her parents' attention had been taken up with the twins and now her friends were all massive Dina-May fans. Lexi was starting to feel invisible. Why couldn't things go her way for once? She screwed up her face and let tears roll silently down her cheeks.

③ Distracted

Over the next few weeks, Lexi gave every spare minute she had to practising her routines for the gymnastics competition. Not only did she work hard in PE and at Miss Barton's after-school sessions, but she practised most evenings on the grass outside the block of flats where she lived. She practised at the park while her mum pushed the twins around in their buggy and walked the dog. Her mum didn't even ask what Lexi was doing. She even practised flipping on to the living room sofa so she could test the tape that held her hearing aid in place.

The day before the competition, Lexi walked to school picturing the final moments of her floor routine. Raising herself on to her toes, she imagined her final run across the mat.

Her speed was perfect. She saw herself cartwheeling, landing and then leaping up into a straddle jump before finishing with a perfect aerial. Finally, this imaginary Lexi landed without a wobble and raised up her arms with outstretched fingertips. Perfect.

"Boo!" shouted Sara, jerking Lexi out of her daydream with a tap on her back.

Lexi hadn't raced Sara to school for weeks. Her embarrassing outburst in the playground over Dina-May had ended up breaking Sara's glasses. They were special ones she needed to stop words moving about on the page when she was reading.

Lexi had apologised, but Sara had looked so sad and bleary-eyed, Lexi wasn't sure if Sara still liked her much after that. It had taken two weeks for Sara to get a new pair of glasses, which had made it difficult for her to read anything in class.

"You know we're all coming to support you and the team tomorrow, don't you?" said Sara, beaming.

"I know," said Lexi. "Thanks." She gave a small smile.

Mrs Wilde had ordered enough coaches so that all the junior classes could come and support the team.

Lexi and Sara walked without talking for a while.

"Your new glasses look good," said Lexi, at last.

"I really like them," said Sara. "The blue tint on the lenses is much better than on my old pair."

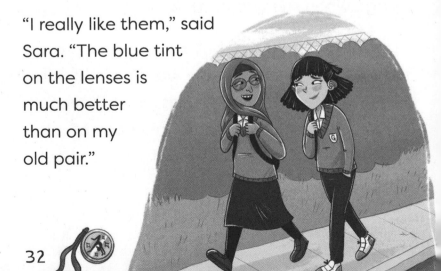

Things seemed to be almost okay between the friends until Sara mentioned the one person Lexi didn't want to talk about.

"I think with you and Dina-May on the team, Greenwicks has a great chance in the competition," Sara said as they headed into the playground.

"You do know Dina-May has loads of proper gym equipment in her garden at home, don't you?" Lexi snapped. "And her parents have two cars and she gets to go to extra gymnastics sessions – even at weekends."

"I know," said Sara, frowning. "But that doesn't make her a horrible person."

"So what does it make her?" Lexi demanded.

Sara thought about it for a second.

"Just lucky, I guess," she said. "At least for having those things." Sara paused.

"But she told us she'd really like a dog and a little brother or sister but she doesn't have either of them and you do."

Lexi wasn't sure what any of that had to do with Dina-May being snooty. And anyway, what did Dina-May think was so great about having a little brother and sister? Since the twins were born, it felt like Lexi wasn't special enough to be noticed in her family. Gymnastics had been the one thing in school where Lexi might have stood out and now even that had been taken away from her.

Dina-May was just better because her parents could afford to send her to a proper club. Tomorrow, everyone would know how amazing Dina-May was when she won everything and led the team to victory.

It's not fair! Lexi thought to herself. She felt a pounding in her head and clenched her fists.

"We're still friends you and me, aren't we?"
Sara asked with a frown.

Lexi didn't answer. She was staring at a
shiny car in the school car park. It wasn't
so unusual, but the tall
man stepping out of
it had caught her
attention.

Sara followed
her gaze.
"That's the man
Mrs Wilde was
showing around a
few weeks ago," she
said.

"The one who said you were really good
when he saw you on the bars," Sara went on.
"I wonder what he's doing here again."

When Sara's back was turned, Lexi quickly ran into school. She hadn't answered Sara's question about whether they were still friends. She'd wanted to make up but she hadn't known what to say.

That lunchtime, Lexi was trying to practise her cartwheels and aerials on the school field as usual, but it was hard to focus. So many children were standing around and watching the man in the tracksuit and a woman in sporty leggings laying out cones and making notes on a clipboard.

Lexi tried to block everything out and focus on her routines. She was just about to cartwheel off the outside balancing beam when she was distracted by a younger child running towards her.

As she spun around in the air, Lexi knew her rotation was all wrong and she landed awkwardly.

"Ow!"

A sharp pain shot through Lexi's ankle and she collapsed to the ground.

"Lexi, are you all right?" asked Sara, running over and kneeling down beside her.

It wasn't long before all Lexi's friends started gathering around her.

"Stand back everyone, please," said Mr Tilton, one of the lunchtime supervisors, making his way through.

"Carter, could you go to the medical room for the ice pack, please?" Mr Tilton asked. "Make sure you *walk*. We don't want any more accidents today."

He knelt down and spoke quietly to Lexi.

"I saw you fall, Lexi," he said kindly. "It's a good job you didn't bang your head. Otherwise, this clowning around might have led to something much worse."

Much worse? Much worse than what? Lexi felt panic rising up in her. What if she was injured? Too injured to compete at tomorrow's competition? And what did Mr Tilton mean by clowning around? She was deadly serious about gymnastics.

Mr Tilton helped Lexi sit up. He asked her if she was hurt and who her teacher was.

Lexi knew Mr Tilton was just checking to make sure she was feeling all right.

"Got it!" Carter panted, running up and handing Mr Tilton the ice pack.

"That was quick!" said Mr Tilton, giving Carter a questioning look.

Lexi shuddered when she felt the pack against her ankle.

When she was ready, Mr Tilton helped her up.

"Did that hurt?" he asked when he saw Lexi wince a little.

"Only a bit," she said, nervously.

"I think you might have sprained your ankle," said Mr Tilton. "Let's take you to the medical room and ask Miss Barton for her opinion."

"But Lexi can't sprain her ankle now!" said Carter. "She needs it for the competition."

Lexi noticed Dina-May was watching with a serious look on her face. *She's probably thinking how she's sure to win gold in the floor routine now,* she thought to herself, pulling a face.

When Lexi got to the medical room, Miss Barton frowned.

"Come on, Lexi," she said quietly. "Let's have a look at your ankle."

Miss Barton got her to sit down and take her shoes and socks off. Then she asked Lexi if she could touch the ankle that hurt.

"I'll be very gentle," she said. "I promise."

When Miss Barton moved her ankle, Lexi found that it tickled more than hurt. She asked Lexi to compare the size of her ankles.

"What do you mean?" asked Lexi. "They're the same."

40

"Exactly," said Miss Barton. "If you had sprained your ankle badly, it would have swollen up."

"So, will I be alright for the competition tomorrow?" asked Lexi. "I have to be, Miss Barton. It's really important!"

Miss Barton let out a long sigh.

"We'll have to see how your foot is tomorrow," she said. "We don't want to make it worse. I think you should definitely miss our practice this afternoon and rest it."

Lexi's eyes were already welling up with tears. Half the school was coming tomorrow – and loads of parents, including her dad. It was her chance to show her parents what she could do, but she was going to be a complete failure.

How could she have been so stupid?

4 Competition Day

It was the morning of the inter-school gymnastics competition.

"How are you feeling, Lexi?" asked Femi. The friends were waiting to get on to the coach along with everyone in Mr Ali's class.

"I feel sick," said Lexi. "And I keep waiting to feel a pain in my ankle."

"No one can tumble and twist like you, Lexi," said Sara. "You're awesome."

"But there might be some better gymnasts coming from other schools," said Carter.

"Thanks for that, Carter," said Femi, pulling a face. "I'm sure that's just what Lexi wants to hear."

For Lexi, the one good thing about yesterday's accident had been seeing how much her friends cared about her.

She looked along the queue of kids for Dina-May and saw her chatting away with Brianna and Leon. All Lexi wanted was to beat Dina-May in the floor competition. A medal would be perfect. At least then, she'd have something to show her mum and dad and all their attention would be on Lexi for once.

"Right," said Miss Barton, ready with her clipboard. "Let's get the team onto the bus first."

It took ages to load up the buses. It wasn't just because Miss Barton had to tick everyone off her list. It was all the other stuff too. Dropped sandwiches, missing first aid kits, forgotten inhalers – even sick bags and a bucket.

"So, how are your parents getting there?" asked Sara, taking the seat next to Lexi.

Lexi hadn't planned to sit with Sara but was glad to see a friendly face.

Lexi shrugged. "Dad said he'd try to get a lift, so he might not make it," said Lexi. "I think Mum's going to have to stay at home and look after the twins."

Mr Ali appeared at the front of the coach. "Before anyone asks, the coach does have a toilet," he announced. "But the driver has asked that we don't use it."

"So, what do we use?" Carter called out. "The bucket?"

Lots of children laughed.

"But I really need the toilet already," said Leon, who was sitting near the front.

"I don't want to use that bucket," someone else called out.

"Look, no one has to use the bucket," said Mr Ali, taking a deep breath.

Then there was another delay while Leon and a bunch of other children went back to the school to use the toilet.

The drive into London felt like the most boring journey ever. When the coach finally turned into the car park at a huge sports centre, everyone started chatting excitedly.

"This place is massive!" exclaimed Carter.

Lexi couldn't believe how huge the arena was inside. The area for floor routines was the biggest she had ever seen, as well as having all the usual areas for different bars, the vault and the beam.

Mrs Wilde and the other teachers led the excited spectators away to find seats, while Miss Barton and the gymnastics team went down to do some warm-ups and stretches on the mats.

"My mum said she's going to sit with your parents to watch," said Ryan as they stretched out their muscles together and Lexi made sure her hearing aid was firmly secured with tape.

Parents? Lexi looked up into the seating area, which was filling up fast. There were so many people watching, it was hard to pick anyone out.

"Look – there they all are!" said Ryan, pointing.

Lexi was amazed to see that not only her dad had made it, but her mum and the twins were there too!

Now, more than ever, Lexi wanted to do well. She was kicking herself for her stupid accident yesterday at school. She wouldn't be doing all four events, as Miss Barton thought it was best that Lexi focused just on the beam and floor events.

"Your amazing aerials will score highly in the floor routine," Miss Barton had said.

Lexi wasn't so sure. She was so nervous as she waited for the competition to begin, it was hard to tell what she thought about anything. She just didn't want to let anyone down.

At exactly 11 o'clock, the lights went down and a spotlight illuminated a woman in a tracksuit standing by the front row of the stands.

Holding a microphone, she welcomed everyone to the event before revealing a big surprise.

"Today's medals will be presented by a very special celebrity gymnast," she announced. "Please put your hands together for three times British champion, Amanda Webb!"

"Amanda Webb!" gasped Lexi as she shielded her eyes from a moving beam of blinding light. Everyone clapped as the beam landed on the woman standing on the competition floor. Amanda Webb was standing so close to Lexi, she could have been on her team! Everyone in the arena cheered and clapped and whooped. Lexi almost felt sick as feelings of excitement, fear and nervousness whirled inside her.

"Amanda's going to be walking around the hall, keeping her eye on all the events," Miss Barton whispered to Lexi with a wink. Then she spoke to the  whole team: "You've all worked so hard. Don't worry about anyone else around you. It's time to get focused now. Good luck!"

The competition began with a loud hooter. The first two events for Greenwicks Primary were vault and bars, so all Lexi had to do was watch and cheer on her teammates. For each event, the gymnast with the highest score from each school had it counted towards their team's total. It was this total that would decide the medals in the team competition.

Ryan did a brilliant performance on the vault and Dina-May had an excellent bar routine, meaning Greenwicks were in a comfortable second place by the time the competitors stopped for lunch.

"Why don't you ever talk to Dina-May?" Sara asked when Lexi moved away from the rest of the team to eat and chat with her friend. "I mean, it's not like you're shy or anything."

Lexi glanced over at Dina-May, who was sitting with the rest of the team. They all seemed to idolise her.

"We've just never really been friends," mumbled Lexi, not entirely sure how she could explain it.

Straight after lunch, it was Lexi's turn to compete on the beam. Despite her nerves, it was the best routine she had ever done.

"Fantastic job, Lexi," said a grinning Miss Barton when Lexi got back to the team bench. "You will have got a really good score for that."

Dina-May was up next on the beam and her routine was perfect, of course.

"I suppose they'll be putting Dina-May's score forward for the team competition, not mine," Lexi sighed. Sure enough, five minutes later Dina-May's score went up on the master scoreboard.

By the end of three events, Greenwicks were still in second place.

Miss Barton gathered the team round. "All we need now is a really good floor routine from someone and we could win the overall team event," she told them. The excitement was almost too much for any of them to bear.

The floor event was the part of the competition Lexi had been waiting for.

If she could do her best here today, not only could she win an individual medal but maybe she could help her whole school to victory in the team event. There were just a handful of gymnasts left to compete when Lexi walked over to the floor, all eyes in the arena focused on her.

"Good luck, Lexi," called a voice as she approached the mat.

Lexi glanced back and was surprised to see that it had been Dina-May, who was waving and smiling excitedly.

When she got the nod from the head judge, Lexi raised her hands to acknowledge him and stepped out on to the big blue mat.

Lexi quickly checked that her mum and dad were watching, and took a deep breath.

Then she got into her starting position, her heart pounding and her hands shaking. The music began and she launched herself into her routine.

She knew all the moves so well that she could picture them in her mind whenever she wanted. She was instantly lost in the music, with everything going well. All that practice had been worth it! Before she knew it, Lexi found herself turning in the corner of the mat for her final sequence. This was it. She raised herself up on to her toes, hands pointing to the ceiling, and started to run ...

5 Beyond Surprised

This was the sequence of moves Lexi had been working on for weeks. Her run-up speed felt perfect. She cartwheeled and landed well, but as she did, Lexi felt a sudden twinge in her ankle.

Ignore it! she thought, as she pushed off for the leap that would lead into the final aerial. But Lexi's push-off lacked the power she needed. She quickly realised that her legs hadn't lifted high enough. Then as she landed, she felt a sharp pain shoot up through her ankle. Immediately, Lexi tried to take some of the weight off that foot by leaning onto her other leg. It was a mistake. The crowd gasped.

Lexi wobbled and toppled forwards, falling out of the performance area.

She crashed flat on to the mat, her ankle throbbing. Her face burned as she looked across at her teammates in panic. What should she do?

"Lexi, forget the final sequence. Do you think you can just finish?" she heard Miss Barton whisper from the bench.

Lexi wanted to disappear. This wasn't like a mistake in practice. Falling over in front of her mum and dad and so many other people was totally devastating. Bravely, she dragged herself up to her feet, turned to the judges and quickly raised her arms to show she'd finished. The crowd and all her team applauded her wildly, but Lexi knew she'd blown it.

As Lexi tried to hobble back to the team bench, a figure dashed out to help her. It was Dina-May.

"Lexi, you were so good!" said Dina-May. "Don't worry about the end – I'm sure you're still going to get a great score."

But Lexi wasn't listening. There was no way now that her performance would count towards anything. She was just Lexi, the class comedian, only she wasn't even funny any more. She was just this sad, pathetic loser. Lexi felt her face turn red and she glared at the floor, desperately trying not to cry.

Sitting on the bench, Lexi realised that Dina-May had her arm around her shoulder.

Lexi didn't shrug it off. Together they watched the next gymnast competing, knowing now that any chance of Greenwicks winning a team medal depended on how Dina-May performed.

"You know Lexi, you are so brave for standing up and finishing the routine," Dina-May whispered. "Whenever I've been injured, even just a little bit, I lose all my confidence completely." Lexi looked up at her and saw Dina-May's face was full of concern.

Finally, it was Dina-May's turn to take to the floor. Lexi was surprised to find herself actually willing her to do well.

"Go on, Dina-May!" she shouted with her teammates.

"Nice to see you two finally getting on," whispered Miss Barton, as Dina-May took up her starting position.

Dina-May was an excellent gymnast but the floor was her weakest event. Lexi guessed she wasn't hoping to win an individual medal in this event. Sure enough, when Dina-May saw her score, she smiled and raised her hands up in a goofy shrug.

Lexi twisted her hands in her lap as they waited for the overall results to come in. Her eyes kept darting to the scoreboard.

Then she gasped. "We got a silver team medal!" she cried, punching the air as she pointed at the final scoreboard. "I never expected that!" Everyone on the Greenwicks bench cheered.

Soon all twelve members of the Greenwicks team were stepping on to the podium to receive their medals. Lexi found herself beaming as she stood there, side by side with everyone, even Dina-May.

"Your teacher told me about your ankle sprain," said Amanda Webb when she put Lexi's silver medal around her neck. "But most of that floor routine was fantastic. Well done!" Lexi held her head up and grinned at the famous athlete, her eyes shining.

All the parents came down to congratulate the school team before they got back on the bus.

"Lexi, you were so brilliant," said her mum, giving her daughter a hug.

"We wouldn't have missed this for the world!" said her dad, his face beaming as he rocked the twins in their double-buggy.

"But how did you all get here?" asked Lexi.

"Have you met my dad?" Dina-May asked, pointing up at the man who had his arm proudly around her shoulder.

Lexi was beyond surprised. Of all the families to help her mum and dad out, it had been Dina-May's!

"Dina-May's dad has also really kindly offered to give you lifts to your old club on Tuesdays if you'd like to start again," said Mum.

"Oh, will you come?" asked Dina-May. "Please – it would be so good to go together!"

As Lexi nodded in confusion and amazement, she wondered if there were any more surprises in store. She didn't have to wait long to find out.

The very next day, there was a buzz going around the playground before school.

"Have you seen what's out on the field?" Carter asked when he saw Lexi and Sara arrive.

Lexi took in all the obstacles and climbing apparatus laid out on the field, and a huge grin spread across her face.

"That looks right up your street, Lexi," said Femi, staring at it all in amazement.

First thing that morning, Mrs Wilde held an assembly and invited the gymnastics team up to the front so their silver medals could be celebrated. As everyone clapped, Lexi saw the tall man in the red tracksuit standing at the back of the hall. After everyone had sat down, Mrs Wilde asked him to come and stand alongside her at the front.

"Now, I'm sure you've all been wondering who this gentleman is and why he and his team have been busy on the school field lately," she started.

Everyone was quiet as they waited for the headteacher to say more.

"This is Joe," Mrs Wilde went on. "All that wonderful apparatus you saw this morning is here for sports week. You're going to be learning parkour, which is also called free-running!"

Joe explained how he and his team would be teaching them basic parkour skills for sports week. He showed them a video of some amazing athletes running, jumping and climbing across a city landscape.

"That looks so cool," murmured Lexi with a dreamy look on her face.

Lexi wasn't sure if Joe heard her, but then he smiled and pointed at her, saying, "I know at least one of you who is going to be amazing at parkour!"

"He means Lexi!" said Carter loudly, giving Sara a nudge.

"She knows, Carter," hissed Sara, rolling her eyes and then giggling. "We all do!"

"I have another bit of exciting news to share with you," Mrs Wilde added to finish off the assembly. "The governors and I have asked Joe to start a new after-school parkour club right here at Greenwicks Primary School after half-term. So, if you enjoy sports week, you won't have to stop there."

Lexi turned to Dina-May. "We have to do it together!"

Dina-May grinned. "Totally."

 Lexi smiled back at her new friend. She couldn't wait to start.

Chat about the book

1 Look at Chapter 1. Why wasn't Lexi attending her gymnastics club for the past year?

2 Read page 21. Lexi was 'mortified' when Dina-May caught her looking at her. What does 'mortified' mean?

3 Go to page 52. Why was the floor event the event Lexi had been waiting for?

4 On page 26, Lexi is described as a 'ticking time bomb'. What does this tell us about her? How do you know?

5 Why is, 'She raised herself up on to her toes, hands pointing to the ceiling and started to run ...' an effective way to end Chapter 4?

6 Read page 33 and 34. What did Lexi and Sara think about Dina-May?

7 Do you think Dina-May and Lexi will be friends after the end of the story? Why?

8 Did you sympathise with Lexi or do you think she behaved badly towards Dina-May when she arrived at Greenwicks Primary School?